LAURENT DE BRUNHOFF

BABAR'S
Book of Color

HARRY N. ABRAMS, INC., PUBLISHERS

One morning when Babar was in his studio, his children Flora, Pom, and Alexander came to see him, bringing Cousin Arthur.

"Can we use some of your paints, Papa?" Pom asked. "We want to paint, too."

RED

"I want red," Flora said and painted two red cherries to hang on her ears.

"I want red, too," said Alexander, "so I can paint a lobster."

BLUE

"My favorite color is blue," said Pom, and he painted a pale blue sky over a big blue whale in the great blue ocean.

YELLOW

"I'm going to paint myself a whole swarm of yellow jackets," said Alexander.

WHITE

"What will you paint with white? Don't forget white," said Babar.

"Snow!" said Alexander.

"A polar bear," said Pom.

"A snow elephant," said Flora.

"And what will you paint with black?" asked Babar.
"A black cat," said Arthur.
"Blackbirds," said Alexander.

"Of course," said Babar. "Why don't each of you pick a color—red, blue, yellow, white, or black—and paint what it makes you think of."

BLACK

"Excellent work!" said Babar. "Now I will show you how to make more colors from just the ones you have." He blew up three balloons—one red, one yellow, one blue.

"Look!" he said, pulling two balloons together. "If you mix two colors you get a third. If you mix all three you get black. Let me see what you can do when you mix colors together."

GREEN

Pom mixed yellow with his favorite, blue, and made green, which he and Flora used to paint frogs and crocodiles.

ORANGE

Flora gave Alexander some red to mix with his yellow. This gave them a bright orange for painting pumpkins.

PURPLE

Last they mixed red and blue to get purple, a beautiful color for a car for Queen Celeste.

GRAY

Babar suggested that Flora add a little black to some white. She was delighted to find she had gray.
  "Now I can paint a big herd of elephants," she said.

PINK

"And now try adding a little red to the white, Flora," said Babar.

"Pink," she said. "Lovely, lovely pink! I've always wanted pink flamingos on my walls."

BROWN

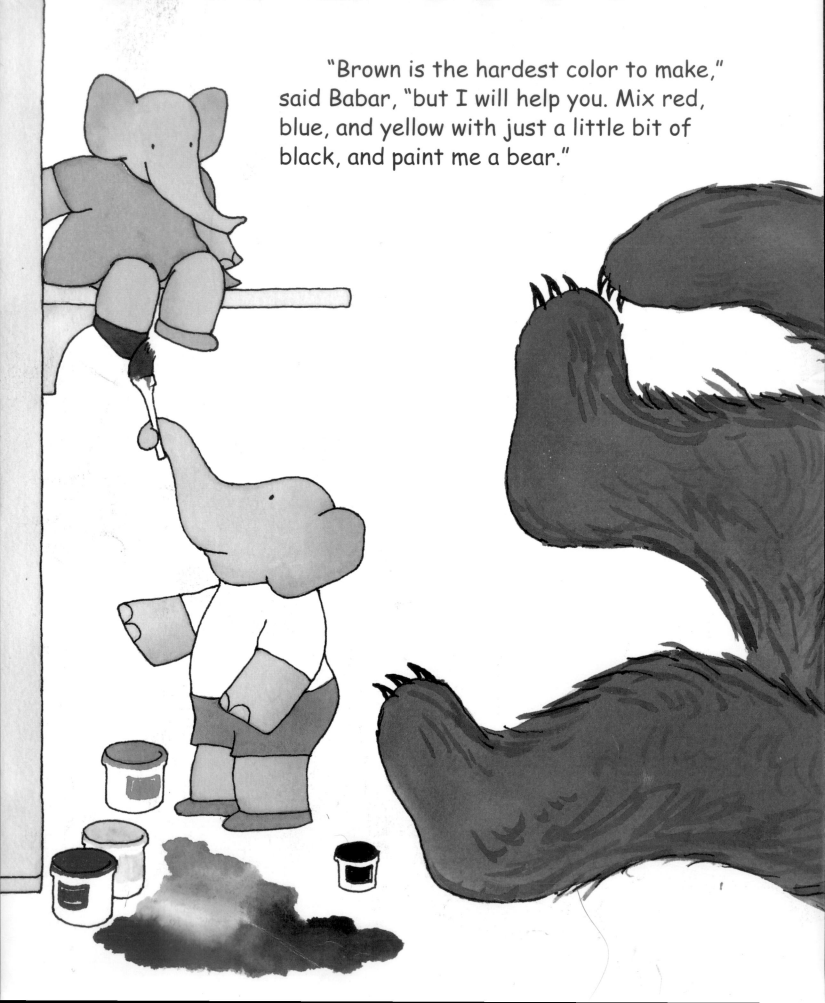

"Brown is the hardest color to make," said Babar, "but I will help you. Mix red, blue, and yellow with just a little bit of black, and paint me a bear."

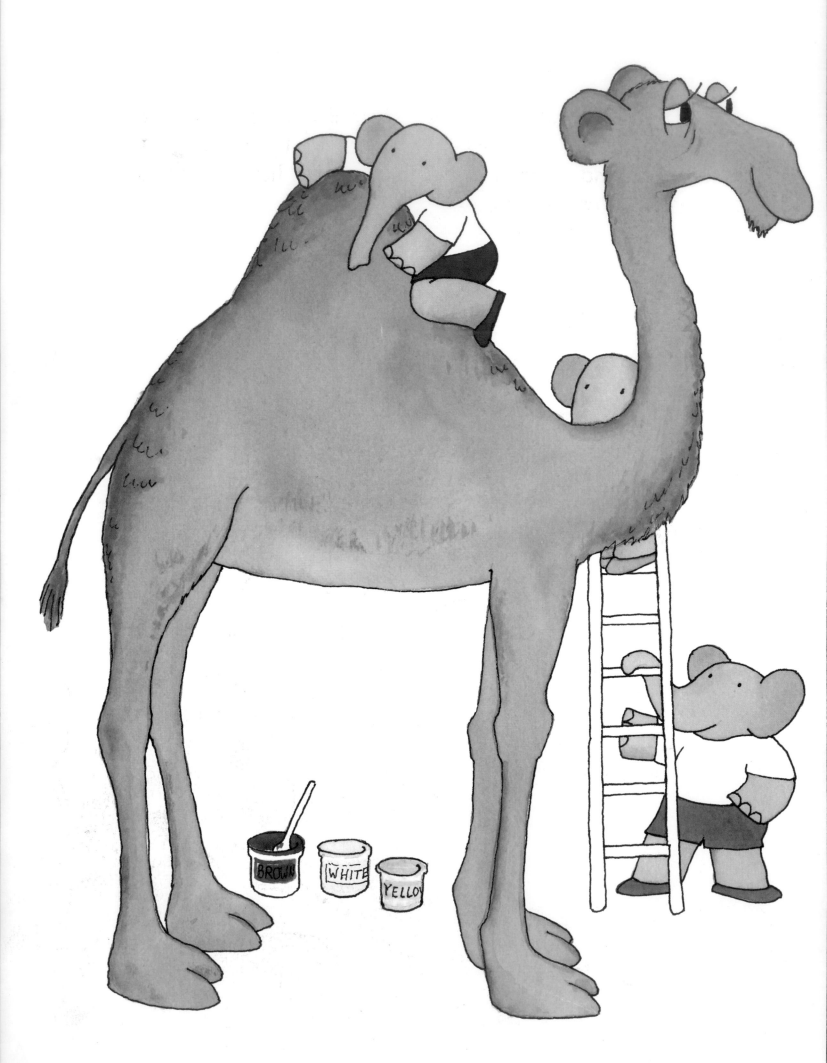

"I'll give you one more color," said Babar, "but then we have to get ready for dinner. Mix the brown you made with a little yellow and a dash of white and you will have tan and can paint yourselves camels."

What a pleasant afternoon
they had playing with color.
Babar hung the artwork on a
display board in his studio,
making the children very proud.

Library of Congress Cataloging-in-Publication-Data

Brunhoff, Laurent de, 1925-
Babar's Book of Color / Laurent de Brunhoff.
p. cm.
Summary: Pom, Flora, Alexander, and Arthur go to Babar' studio
and learn about mixing and using colors.

ISBN 0-8109-4840-0
[1. Color—Fiction. 2. Elephants—Fiction.] I. Title.

PZ7.B82843Babj 2004
[E]—dc22

2003013235

First published in 1984. Published in 2004 by Harry N. Abrams, Incorporated, New York

Printed and bound in China

10 9 8 7 6 5 4 3 2

Harry N. Abrams, Inc.
100 Fifth Avenue
New York, N.Y. 10011
www.abramsbooks.com

Abrams is a subsidiary of
LA MARTINIÈRE
GROUPE